MY
MAGICAL
PONY TALES
COLLECTION

INTRODUCTION

There is something magical about ponies. They can move as swiftly as the wind. They are strong but they are gentle. They show what they are thinking in hundreds of ways, yet they are always mysterious.

This collection of magical pony tales is as varied as ponies themselves. The stories will make you wonder and wish, laugh and cry, smile and sigh. There are ponies who make dreams come true and ponies who are just as foolish as the silliest human being. But all of these extraordinary ponies are magical in one way or another.

Look very carefully and you will find other surprises in these pages as well. At least one lucky horseshoe is hidden on each page of the book.

Can you find the hidden horseshoes?
How many can you see?
Remember, the more that you can find
The luckier you will be!

MY
MAGICAL
PONY TALES
COLLECTION

Illustrated by
CATHIE SHUTTLEWORTH

Written by
NICOLA BAXTER

mjf
media

This special edition printed
exclusively for MJF Media
© 2001 Bookmart Limited

1 3 5 7 9 10 8 6 4 2

First published by Armadillo Books
an imprint of Bookmart Limited
Registered Number 2372865
Trading as Bookmart Limited
Blaby Road, Wigston
Leicestershire, LE18 4SE

ISBN 978-1-84322-542-3

Produced for Bookmart Limited by Nicola Baxter
PO Box 215
Framingham Earl
Norwich Norfolk
NR14 7UR

Designer: Amanda Hawkes
Editor: Jenny Knight
Editorial consultant: Ronne Randall

Printed in China

CONTENTS

The Magical Tale of

The Pony of the North Wind

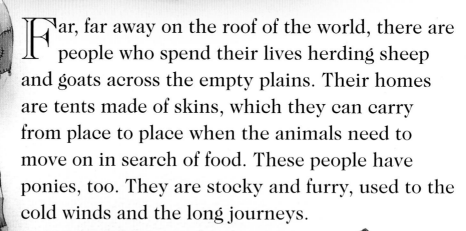

Far, far away on the roof of the world, there are people who spend their lives herding sheep and goats across the empty plains. Their homes are tents made of skins, which they can carry from place to place when the animals need to move on in search of food. These people have ponies, too. They are stocky and furry, used to the cold winds and the long journeys.

But it is not of these ponies that the grandmothers tell the little ones, when they are all huddled around the fire at night. They speak of the pony of the north wind—a white pony with a flowing mane and tail, whose hoofs are of silver and so light they hardly make a sound upon the cold earth. This is the pony of the north wind. This is the pony that brings the snow.

"You must listen, my children," say the grandmothers, "and look out at the sky. When the clouds are heavy and dull and the wind begins to moan, listen hard for the sound of silver hoofs. It is like no other sound you will ever hear. It is in the silence when the wind is still for a moment. It is in the breathing of the beasts as they shift and stray. It is in the beating of your hearts. When you hear those silver hoofs, you must pitch your tents and stay close to your mothers. For the north wind is galloping and bringing the snow."

The children smiled at what the grandmothers said. Spring was coming. It seemed a long, long time before the pony of the north wind would gallop by their tents again.

"I don't believe there is such a pony," said a little boy called Ula. "Ponies don't have silver hoofs. They can't move along without making a sound. I don't believe it at all."

The grandmothers shivered and shook their heads. They didn't like to hear someone speak so of something he did not understand.

Spring came at last. It was still cold on the wide, open plains, and the winds blew as strongly as ever, but the stocky little ponies that grazed around the camps became sleeker. The sparse,

tough grass grew a little longer. The sheep and goats looked healthy and plump. Soon little lambs and kids were standing with their mothers, testing their wobbly legs on the hard, flat ground. The children helped the herders to keep the little ones safe from wild dogs and lions.

Summer swept over the plains leaving scarcely a trace. Only a few shy flowers nodded their tiny heads in the sunlight. The wild wind never stopped. It ruffled the manes of the ponies and battered at the tents, begging to be let in. Inside, safe and warm in the light evenings, the old women began to talk of the autumn and the cold. It was coming, they said. They could feel it in their bones.

"It is time we were moving south again," they said. "For the cold winds are coming closer every day."

Once again the herds moved on and the
herders with them. The children's red cheeks
glowed in the freshening wind. Their black hair
streamed out behind them as they ran beside the
animals. The little brown ponies lowered their
heads and hunched their shoulders against the
cold. The nights grew darker.

It was a little girl who first noticed that the boy
Ula had gone. With watering eyes, she stared
across the plains, but there was no sign of him.
The grandmothers hung their heads and sighed.
No one could survive by himself in the weather
that was coming.

"We warned him," they said. "For him,
knowledge will come too late."

Far away, alone on the wind-whipped plain,
Ula heard his own heart beating. It frightened him.
He listened to the moaning of the wind and
thought he heard … something … a pulse, a beat,
a drumming on the earth. He knelt and put his ear
to the hard ground, hoping to pick up the sound of
his own people and find the direction they had
gone. But all he could hear was his own breath,
hot against his hand, and the thudding of his own
heart, fast and fearful.

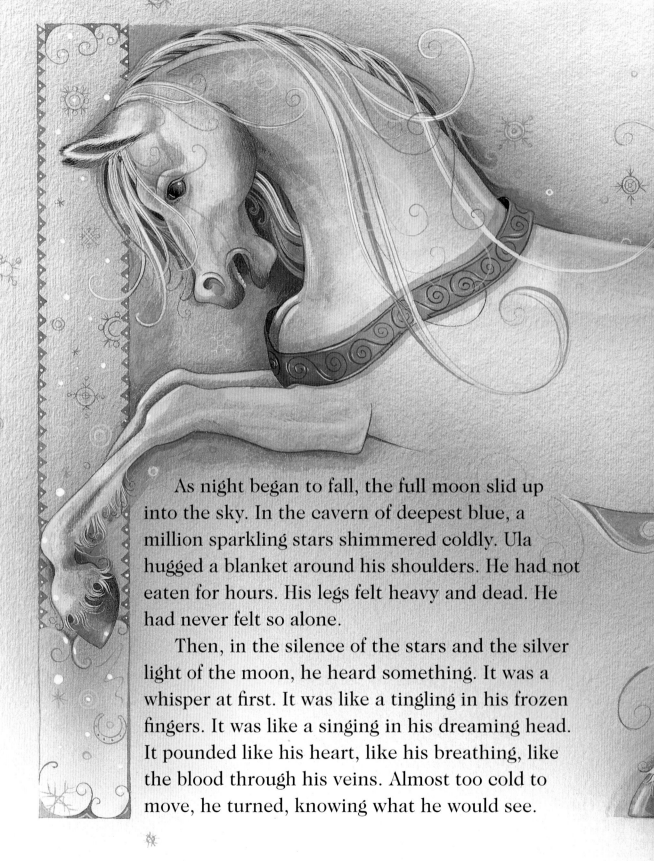

As night began to fall, the full moon slid up into the sky. In the cavern of deepest blue, a million sparkling stars shimmered coldly. Ula hugged a blanket around his shoulders. He had not eaten for hours. His legs felt heavy and dead. He had never felt so alone.

Then, in the silence of the stars and the silver light of the moon, he heard something. It was a whisper at first. It was like a tingling in his frozen fingers. It was like a singing in his dreaming head. It pounded like his heart, like his breathing, like the blood through his veins. Almost too cold to move, he turned, knowing what he would see.

The pony of the north wind was fearsome. It moved like the lashing of a winter storm. Its hoofs made no sound on the earth, but little bright sparks flew up where they struck. Its mane streamed out behind it, cold as ice and furious as flame. But its eyes … its eyes were glinting with cold. Ula looked into them and felt his blood freeze. He closed his pale eyes and dropped to the ground like a falling star. He was still.

Behind the pony came the snow. Soft, white flakes covered the boy, wrapping him safe in a blanket of snow. And the pony of the north wind swept on over the plain, catching the herders in their tents, chilling the grandmothers as they huddled by the fire, making their dark eyes fill with tears as they grieved for the boy who was lost.

But Ula didn't feel the cold. The icy wind passed through him and he smiled. His spirit soars in the wind now. He lives in the moaning of the wind and the sighing of the stars. And he rides the pony of the north wind, never sorry, never still.

The Enchanted Tale of
THE FOREST PONIES
OF ELFLAND

Elves, as you know, are tiny. They can drink from acorn cups and fill their quilts with thistledown. Their ponies are tiny too, by human standards, but they are much, much bigger than elves. No elf would dream of trying to ride an Elfland pony. Those little people are much more at home perched on the back of a large frog, or a duck, or a rabbit. They twist grasses together to make little bridles and sew leaves together to make saddles. Then up they hop and off they go, with a hop, a waddle, or a jump.

Meanwhile, deep in the forests, the Elfland ponies are hardly ever seen, even by elves. They are completely wild and very shy. Some are a leafy shade of green. Others are dappled brown and yellow and green, like the patterns that sunlight makes when it splashes through the trees.

You could easily walk through an Elfland forest and never see a pony, although dozens of them might be standing quietly by the path, blending with the leaves and branches.

Almost everything in Elfland is magic. The ponies are no exception, but they only use their magic when their country and the elves that live there are threatened. That is what happened when the Wizard of Marr turned his hideous attention towards Elfland.

The Wizard of Marr was evil through and through. Everything his twisted fingers touched died or became ugly. When the goblins rose up and threw him out of his castle on Brooding Peak, he decided to travel across the mountains into Elfland. He hated elves. They were, in his opinion, weak creatures, too nice for their own good.

The elves first knew about the arrival of the Wizard of Marr when a horrible dusty wind blew into their homes and covered everything in a layer of thick, evil-smelling ash. The wizard had set fire to the wonderful rolling wheatfields that stretched from the foot of the mountains to the edge of the forests. Before long, the elves could smell the burning from their tree-trunk homes.

"If the flames reach the forest, we are finished," said Elderberry. "What can we possibly do?"

"We can beat out the flames with sticks and carry water from our wells," said Holly bravely. But she knew that it was hopeless.

Nevertheless, the next morning, a band of twenty little elves set out. The Wizard of Marr, viewing them through his magic telescope, laughed softly. With a wave of his hand, he put out the flames, leaving an ugly burnt path to show where he had been.

Above the little party of elves, the smoky air cleared. Elderberry scrambled to the top of a tree and looked out over the fields.

"The fire has stopped," he said, "but a huge black cloud is moving this way. Let's go back to our homes. Quickly!"

No sooner had the elves shut themselves into the hollowed-out houses than a frightening storm exploded overhead. Thunder rattled the windows. Lightning crackled alarmingly. And rain lashed at the forest like arrows from a furious army. The elves huddled in their homes, watching as leaves and branches blew past outside.

"Such a storm has never been known in
Elfland," said Holly's father, Hawthorn. "We can't
take much more of this. I've been thinking. This
storm isn't natural, you know. Some evil force is
attacking us, and there is nothing that we can do
about it. Look out!"

A huge branch hurtled through the window
and missed the little family by inches. Through
the broken panes, the rain lashed viciously at
everything it could touch. Between the roaring of
the thunder and the snapping of the lightning,
another sound could be heard. It was low and soft.
It made the hair stand up on the back of your
neck and cold trickles run down your spine. It was
a while before the elves realized what it was.
Someone was laughing.

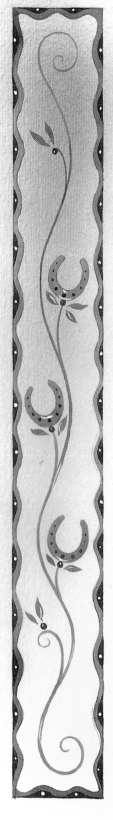

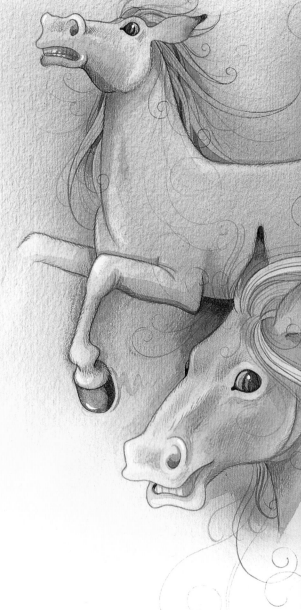

All this time, the ponies had been shifting restlessly in the forest. Their keen nostrils smelled the smoke and they shied nervously. When the storm came, they huddled under the trees, their heads resting on each other's backs.

But as the Wizard of Marr drew closer, the ponies felt his evil. They could sense the sick sweetness of his magic slithering across the mossy ground towards them. They lifted their heads and faced the enemy.

There was no signal. There was no sound. But suddenly the ponies began to move as one, galloping towards the source of the danger like a green, foaming sea. Their thudding hoofs drowned the thunder. Their tossing manes shook off the rain. Faster and faster they galloped, brushing lightly past the elves' homes on the edge of the forest, surging towards the mountains, feeling the wizard's evil closer with every step.

The Wizard of Marr, laughing in the face of the storm and thinking only of the harm that he could do, did not notice the ponies until it was too late. Suddenly, their hoofs were on the hem of his robes. He felt their hot breath on his cheek. But he could not see them. His twisted mind refused to see the tide of goodness that swept towards him. All he felt was a terrible faintness as his power drained from him.

That evening, all was still in the forests of Elfland. In the glow of the setting sun, the elves began to repair the damage that the storm had done. Deep in the forest, the ponies melted into the shadows once more. And at the foot of the mountains, a very old and feeble man in tattered robes began to climb.

The Spellbinding Tale of

THE PURPLE DREAM PONY

There are, as I'm sure you know, mountain ponies and forest ponies. There are ponies who race across the wide plains or swim the foaming rivers between rolling, green hills.

But there are also ponies who do not live anywhere in the real world. They are dream ponies, who carry sleeping children to the land of dreams and bring them safely home again when morning comes.

Dream ponies are beautiful. They have long, flowing manes and tails. Their coats are in lovely jewel shades of sapphire, emerald, amethyst and topaz. Their hoofs sparkle like diamonds, but their eyes are soft and kind.

Young dream ponies must learn to take very good care of the children they carry.

"Never let them become frightened," say the older ponies, "by galloping too fast. Take them to the sweetest dreams you can find. And make sure you take them home in plenty of time."

The purple dream pony, ready for her first real mission, listened carefully to these words.

That evening, as the soft dusk fell over the fields, the purple dream pony set off to find the child she would carry to the land of dreams. She waited patiently outside his window, knowing that she must not let him see her while he was still awake.

At last Tom—that was his name—put down his book and closed his eyes. The purple pony entered his room by magic and stood quietly by his bed. Then she gently asked him what kind of dream he would like to have that night.

Tom didn't hesitate. "A dream about castles," he said, "and knights on horseback."

"Climb onto *my* back," smiled the purple pony, "and I'll take you there."

Off they galloped, flying through the night towards a shimmering place among the stars.

"A castle!" cried Tom. "Let me get down and explore! It's just like the one in my book!"

The purple dream pony watched as the little boy ran through the castle, pretending to be a brave knight. She made sure that she could see where he was all the time. It was her job to make sure that this was a good dream.

Tom played all night long. He had a wonderful time. The purple dream pony felt that she was doing a good job. But suddenly, as she looked at the castle, she saw a terrible thing. A rosy light was glowing on the stone wall. The purple dream pony whirled around. Behind her, the sun was beginning to rise, flooding the sky with a pinkish orange light. Dawn was coming and Tom was not yet home!

The purple dream pony did not waste a second. She scooped the little boy up onto her back and set off through the glow of early morning.

"But I don't want to go!" wailed Tom. "I was having such a good time!"

The pony felt frightened now. Dreams are wonderful things, but every dream pony must make sure that waking up to a whole new day is just as much fun. No one can live in dreamland all the time.

The purple dream pony flew like the wind. She had to get Tom back to his bed before he awoke and saw her. Birds were singing loudly in Tom's garden as the pony landed gently under his window. The pony was only just in time. As Tom's head hit the pillow, his eyelids began to flutter. He stretched and yawned.

In the daylight, the dream pony faded. You could hardly see her now as she waited anxiously beside Tom's bed. Then the little boy woke up properly and smiled as a delicious smell wafted into the room.

"Pancakes for breakfast!" he cried happily. It was a wonderful dream, but I'm *so* glad to be awake!"

The dream pony sighed with relief—and like the darkness, she faded right away.

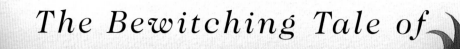

The Bewitching Tale of

THE PRINCESS PONY

When King Hippus struck the ground with his royal hoof, everyone knew he was very cross indeed. When he tossed his mane and let his crown slip over one eye, the other magical ponies shuffled nervously. What was annoying their noble king?

Queen Equestra tried to soothe him.

"My dear," she whinnied gently, "it can't be as bad as that."

"It can and it is!" snorted His Majesty, stamping again. "What did I do to deserve such a tiresome child? She has been nothing but trouble since she stopped being a foal and started being a…"

"A real princess!" his wife interposed quickly. She knew only too well that her husband's royal vocabulary included some quite *impolite* words. "But whatever has she done to upset you now? I've not heard a word from her all day."

"That," snuffled the King, "is the problem."

He looked out of the window of the Royal Stable into the gardens below.

"Look!" he said.

Far below, under a flowering cherry tree, a beautiful young pony sat among the pink blossoms. She sighed. She rubbed her head against the trunk of the tree. She tossed her mane in a girlish way.

"Oh," said the Queen. She understood everything now.

"She won't talk to me at all," said the King. "You know how it is. I thought after the last time…"

The Queen nodded her handsome head. The trouble with the princess pony these days was that she was constantly falling in love … and always with the most unsuitable ponies. At such times, she refused to speak, but she did a lot of head-tossing, sighing and sitting by herself in the garden.

Over the past year, two cart horses, a handsome but unreliable racehorse and a very shifty show jumper had all been sent away to the farthest parts of the kingdom. Each time, the pining princess had been heartbroken for about a day and a half, before another fine fetlock caught her eye.

The Queen hurried down to the garden to find out who was concerned this time. It was so tiresome. She was sure she couldn't remember being such a problem to her parents when *she* was a filly.

The Princess gave another big sigh as her mother approached. The Queen was gentle.

"Now Ponita," she said, "I know why you are moping here like this. Tell me all about it."

The Princess sighed again. "It's Prince Cavallo," she said. "He is *so* wonderful."

"But darling, you are so young," began her mother. Then she stopped. "Just a minute, did you say *Prince* Cavallo?" she asked. "You mean King Canter's son? But, my dear, why didn't you say so? He is such a charming young pony. You must invite him to the Royal Stable at once!"

The King and Queen were delighted. Prince Cavallo was an entirely suitable match for their daughter. The Prince was happy, too.

By the time lunch was over, the King and the Queen and the Prince between them had set the date and time of the wedding and decided on the flowers in the bridal bouquet.

But they had not consulted Princess Ponita. It is one thing to sigh hopelessly for a pony. It is quite another to find that the idea is not hopeless at all. As soon as she saw how well he was getting on with her parents, the Princess lost all interest in her Prince. That evening, she told her parents so.

The King tossed his head until his crown fell right off. He stamped his hoof a lot, too. But the Queen simply smiled.

"Ponita *was* much too young," she said. "We'll do just the same next time."

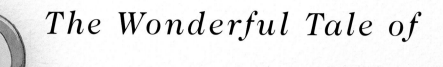

The Wonderful Tale of
THE PONY WHO FLEW

On the gentle, green slopes of the Harmony Hills, a herd of ponies grazed in the sunshine. Every now and then, they lifted their handsome heads and shook their manes in the light breeze, sniffing the soft air. All was well. No danger threatened from near or far.

Only one pony felt uneasy. It was Blue, a silvery stallion with a darker mane and tail. It wasn't because he detected a problem that the other ponies didn't. The opposite was true. Blue was restless *because* everything was fine.

Long ago, when he was a spindly-legged foal, Blue sat beside his old grandfather and listened to stories of long ago. He heard of great battles between the leaders of huge herds. His heart pounded as he heard the story of the Great Journey, when the herd made its way south to find peace and plenty in the Harmony Hills. Many fine ponies were lost along the way. Heroic deeds were done. It was a dreadful, painful and *exciting* time.

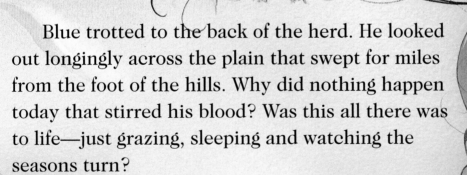

Blue trotted to the back of the herd. He looked out longingly across the plain that swept for miles from the foot of the hills. Why did nothing happen today that stirred his blood? Was this all there was to life—just grazing, sleeping and watching the seasons turn?

Blue's mother tried to calm him. "This is the best place the herd has ever lived," she said. "There are no wolves or lions. The winters are mild and the summer sun shines gently on our backs. This is a safe place for foals to be raised and old horses to live out their lives in peace."

But Blue was still dissatisfied. One day, when the head of the herd was not looking, he trotted off into the hills and was soon lost from view in a deep valley.

The young stallion did not know what he was looking for, but he felt a shiver of fear as the steep slopes on either side hid him from the sun. It was darker and cooler here. A little stream, cold and clear, trickled along the bottom of the valley. Blue trotted beside it.

As he went, the stream widened and became a river. The ground grew rockier. He had to be careful where he placed his feet. More than once, he stumbled and almost fell.

After an hour, Blue was out of breath. At first he thought it was his own blood that roared in his ears. It wasn't until a jet of glistening spray hit his face that he looked up and saw that the thundering came from a massive waterfall, dropping like a glorious, glistening mane from the cliff edge far above. Blue had never seen anything so powerful and extraordinary.

The rushing water seemed to hypnotize the horse gazing up at it. He could not stop looking at it. And it seemed to him that in the rushing water he could see strange shapes. Suddenly, he gasped. For a moment, a rush of water seemed to him like a mighty stallion, leaping through the water, flying through the thunder.

Then Blue knew what he must do. Slowly and painfully he clambered the steep slope beside the cliff. As he climbed, his heart pounded in his chest. He had never felt so tired—or so alive.

At last the silver stallion stood on a rock at the top of the waterfall. He looked down. Surely, he thought, he could fly like the water-stallion, rushing downwards with the tumbling spray. And if he never saw the green hills of home again, at least he would have done one wonderful, extraordinary thing in his short life.

Blue tossed his head and looked up to sniff the air one more time … and all thoughts of flying vanished from his head. The view from so high was breathtaking! Blue could see across the hills and over the plain to the blue hills beyond. He could see down the river to the wide blue sea. He could see the great curving arc of the yellow shore stretching forever on either side.

There was so much more to see! There was so much more to do! The great adventure of Blue's life began right there and then. Although his four hoofs stayed firmly on the ground, his spirit flew.

The Fantastic Tale of

THE PONY OF THE SEA

Once upon a time there was a boy who lived in a village a few miles from the coast. Half the men from the village made their living on the land. The other half were fishermen, risking their lives on the dark and dangerous sea.

Now, the boy in this story, whose name was John, was his mother's only child. She had lost her husband and her own father to the deep waters and was determined that her son should be safe. From his earliest days, she talked to him about farming. She told him how the soft sun warmed the earth in the spring. Gentle rain helped the grass to grow and feed the sheep and cattle. In the fields, crops grew higher and higher, ripening in the summer's heat. Then, at harvest time, the barns were filled with golden grain.

When John was old enough to go to work himself, it seemed natural to turn to the land. He loved the rhythm of the seasons and soon found he had a special talent for looking after the huge horses that pulled the carts and the threshing machines. He loved to see them toss their heads and stamp their mighty hoofs, eager to get to work. Their strength astonished him.

The horses in turn worked well for the young man. He treated them kindly, always making sure that they were comfortable and well fed before he went home for his own supper.

For five years, John worked for one of the rich
farmers who owned all the land in the area. Then
times became hard. The farmer called his workers
together and told them he had to reduce their
wages. Now the boy and his mother had only just
enough to live on.

As winter drew on, a worse difficulty faced the
young man. His mother became ill. The doctor
shook his head and said she needed expensive
medicine, but there was little money to pay for it.
Night after night, John lay awake, worrying about
what to do. There was only one way, he knew, to
make a large sum of money quickly.

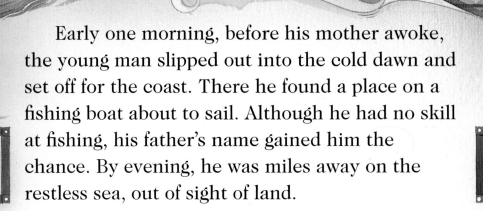

Early one morning, before his mother awoke,
the young man slipped out into the cold dawn and
set off for the coast. There he found a place on a
fishing boat about to sail. Although he had no skill
at fishing, his father's name gained him the
chance. By evening, he was miles away on the
restless sea, out of sight of land.

Life on board the fishing boat was unlike anything the young man had ever known. He longed to feel the solid earth under his feet again. The constant movement of the boat made him ill, and the fishermen laughed when he did not understand the words they used for parts of the boat and the work they did.

But worse was to come. Two days later, the sky grew dark and heavy. The sea heaved, making the boat creak and sway. Frightened by the faces of the fishermen, John begged them to tell him what to do. "Pray," said the skipper.

He was right. The skill of the crew and the strength of the boat were no match for the furious storm. As mountainous waves smashed down onto the boat, John's fingers were torn from the railing he clung to. He felt himself flung into the air, hurtling towards the black, boiling water.

The sea was so cold that the shock of it almost killed him. Half-conscious, he felt himself being dragged below the surface.

Then, suddenly, when he had lost all hope, John felt himself being pushed upwards. It was as though something was supporting him, something with as much strength as the sea. Through half-open eyes, he thought he saw the powerful neck of a giant horse rearing before him, its mane a stinging tangle of whipping spray. As the world grew dark around him, John clasped his arms around the sea-horse and closed his eyes.

It was many hours later that
a girl, walking along the beach
in the calm after the recent
storm, found the young
man lying on the sand.
He was barely alive,
but she ran for
help and had
him carried
to her father's
house.

That was the one and only time that John went
to sea. It happened that the girl was the daughter
of his former master.

"He's a remarkable young man," said the
farmer, looking down at the sleeping youth. "Do
you know that not a horse on the farm has been
willing to work while he's been gone?"

His daughter smiled. She had already made up
her own mind about the lad.

So John is set to become as wealthy a farmer
as his father-in-law. His mother is well and happy
to see her son safe home forever. But at night,
when the winds howl around the farmhouse, John
is quiet and grave, thinking of the poor souls out
upon the stormy seas.

The Mysterious Tale of
THE PONY IN THE MIST

When you live on the edge of a marsh, you can expect a winter of cold and misty weather. Old Meg was used to it. She had lived in her little cottage for over sixty years. When strange white shapes swept across the bleak landscape and clustered around her door, she was not afraid. She lit her lamps and waited until the weather cleared.

During the winter, no one ever came near Old Meg's home. Even local people could not find their way across the treacherous marsh in the fog. A stranger who tried would disappear without trace in the murky pools that lurked beside firmer ground.

Old Meg always made sure that her pantry was full and her log pile was high before the bad weather set in. This year was no exception. On the morning when she looked out of her window and could see nothing at all but the smoky, white mist, she was not at all alarmed.

The winter slowly passed. One night close to Christmas, Old Meg sat before her fire and heard a strange sound outside. She paid no attention. It might be the howling of the wind. It might be an owl swooping like a shadow across the marsh. It could not possibly be a human being.

But above the crackling of the fire, the sound came again. And again. Meg put down her knitting and listened. It sounded extraordinarily like a pony neighing.

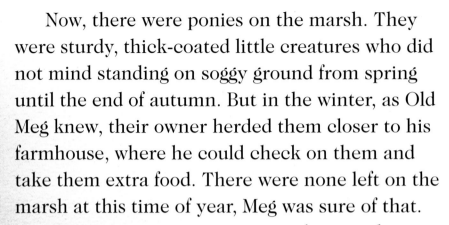

Now, there were ponies on the marsh. They were sturdy, thick-coated little creatures who did not mind standing on soggy ground from spring until the end of autumn. But in the winter, as Old Meg knew, their owner herded them closer to his farmhouse, where he could check on them and take them extra food. There were none left on the marsh at this time of year, Meg was sure of that.

But the sound came again, and Old Meg threw her shawl about her head and opened her door. She could see nothing. Even when she fetched a lantern from inside the house, she could only see the mist swirling around her. Something was there, however. Now that she was outside, the old woman could hear not only the gently neighing but also the shifting of hoofs on the frosty ground. There really was a pony out there— and not very far away.

Old Meg had lived on the marsh too long to

take foolish risks. She feared she would be lost forever if she went out into the mist on her own, so she called to the pony, hoping it would come to her.

The pony did not move. He must be stuck or hurt, the old lady decided. Hurrying back into her cottage, she took a stout stick in one hand and a ball of her knitting yarn in the other. She tied one end of the yarn to the door knocker and set off into the mist, feeling the ground in front of her with her stick, to which she had tied a lantern.

The pony was only a few yards away. He was so much the same shade as the mist he stood in that Meg did not see him until she felt his warm breath on her face. She stretched up her hand to reassure the pony, whose big dark eyes gleamed in the lantern-light.

The pony tossed his head. He did not want to be touched. Instead, he stamped with one hoof on the ground. Old Meg looked down and gasped. Almost under the pony's hoof was a bundle of rags. It looked … no, it couldn't be … it was! There was a baby wrapped inside them.

Old Meg drove her stick into the ground and picked up the baby. She was sure it could not be alive on such a cold night, but when she buried her face in the bundle, the golden hair felt warm. Tucking the child inside her shawl, Old Meg turned to hurry back to her cottage. When she looked over her shoulder, the pony had disappeared, swiftly and silently, into the mist.

Where the tiny baby had come from, Old Meg never knew. She was a beautiful little girl. When the spring came, and the old woman could try to find out, no one could help. So Old Meg, who thought she would never have a daughter of her own, and much to the surprise of those who knew her, raised the child herself.

It was as though a light had come on in the old woman's life. She named the little girl Eleanor, and did everything for her. In the summer, Eleanor crossed the marsh each day to go to school. In the winter, she stayed at home with Old Meg, sitting beside the fire and listening to tales of long ago and far away.

It was on one of those winter evenings that the old woman told her daughter, now almost a young woman, of the mysterious pony of the mist and how she had arrived. She thought Eleanor would be astonished, but the girl simply nodded.

"I wonder," she said, "if the pony that carried me here will take me away one day. If he can bring life, perhaps he can take it."

Old Meg felt a cold fear tighten around her heart. More than anything in the world, she dreaded losing the girl who had brought light and love into her life. One day, she knew, it must happen, but she hoped with all her strength that she would not be alive to see it.

The years passed. Old Meg became very, very frail. "Don't leave me, Eleanor," she begged, when the mist swirled around the cottage once more.

"I will never leave you," promised the girl.

But one night, as they sat in the warmth of the cottage, Old Meg heard a sound that had echoed in her mind for twenty years. Desperately, she began talking, singing, laughing—anything to stop her daughter from hearing what she herself had heard. The old woman did her best, but she was weak. When she paused for breath, the neighing of a pony sounded high and clear in the icy stillness.

Eleanor rose to her feet and looked sadly at her mother. The old woman gazed into her daughter's misty eyes and suddenly smiled. In the firelight, she looked like a girl again herself.

"Oh, I was wrong to be afraid of this moment," she said. "How silly of me! Good-bye, my dear, dear girl. Remember me, wherever you go."

"I will," promised Eleanor, brushing away tears.

Then, still smiling, Old Meg pulled her shawl around her shoulders and walked out into the mist to where a strange and beautiful creature waited.

The Stargazing Tale of

THE PONY OF THE NIGHT

Once upon a time, there was a little pony called Daisy. She loved to kick her heels in the sunshine and gallop up and down the meadow where she lived with her mother and aunt. The older ponies smiled to see the little one so happy.

But as the shadows lengthened in the afternoon, Daisy would become quiet. There was no more rushing about or chasing butterflies. Her head drooped to the darkening green grass and she sighed unhappily.

At first, Daisy's mother, whose name was Billie, thought her daughter might be ill. A little cold perhaps? A funny feeling in her tummy? Daisy shook her head. There was nothing wrong, she said.

"It's just one of those things," said Caramel, Daisy's aunt. "I was the same when I was her age—happy one moment and sad the next. She'll be fine tomorrow."

When the same thing happened, day after day, Billie became more concerned. She took her little daughter over to a shady tree and spoke gently to her.

"You know you can tell me, Daisy, if anything is wrong," she said. "I like to see my girl enjoying herself. What is wrong?"

"Nothing," said Daisy. "Nothing at all."

"Now, Daisy," Billie insisted, "that simply isn't true. You must tell me, however embarrassing or silly it is. I won't mind."

"I'm fine," said Daisy.

Billie let the matter drop, but she had a word with her sister.

"Why don't you try talking to her?" she suggested. "Sometimes a young pony will tell an aunt things she won't tell her mother."

Caramel tried to be cheery about the whole thing, which was probably a mistake.

"Now then, Daisy," she said, "let's not have any more of this nonsense. Tell me what the trouble is and I'll fix it for you."

"You can't," whispered Daisy, and that was all she would say.

"It's a step forward," Caramel told Billie. "At least she admitted there is a problem."

"We knew that before," grunted Billie. "I'm going to have to have stern words with that girl."

Billie didn't mean to be unkind, but she was getting tired of seeing Daisy drooping about for no apparent reason. And she had given her daughter lots of chances to tell her what was going on.

"Now, Daisy," she neighed, tossing her head firmly, "I want to know exactly what the problem is, and I want to know now. If you don't tell me at once, I will be very angry."

Daisy saw that her mother meant business.

"All right," she whinnied. "I'm afraid of the dark. There, now you can laugh!"

Billie snorted. "I'm not laughing, Daisy," she said. "Now I really am angry. No self-respecting horse or pony is afraid of the dark. It's ridiculous. Night is just the same as day—only it's dark. There's nothing to be afraid of. I don't want to hear any more about it."

But Caramel, who was grazing nearby and trying hard to look as if she wasn't eavesdropping, was reminded of something long ago.

"You know," she told her niece, "once I knew a little pony who was frightened just like you. And my mother told her something that meant she was never scared again. She told her about the pony who looks down on all of us at night and makes sure we are safe."

"Where?" asked Daisy. "How? When? Why can't I see her?"

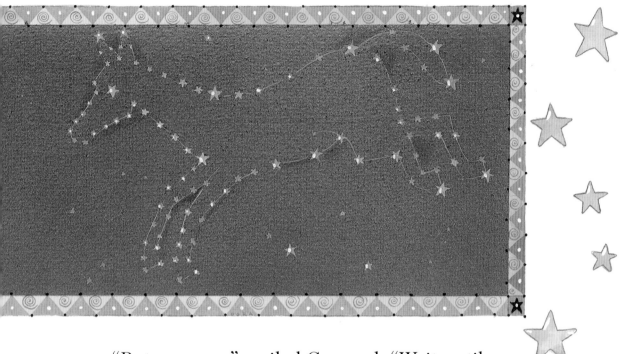

"But you can," smiled Caramel. "Wait until tonight and I'll show you."

That night, when the deep blue sky above was filled with stars, the kind aunt told Daisy to look up.

"I can only see the stars," said Daisy.

"Exactly," replied Caramel. "But if you keep looking long enough, you will see the shape of a pony, picked out in stars. Keep looking!"

Well, Daisy really did want to see the star pony, and, you know, pretty soon she was sure that she could. There it was, looking down on her!

"I don't feel frightened any more," sighed Daisy.

"Neither did the little pony I remember," said Caramel. "Did she, Billie?"

And Daisy's mother was glad that the darkness hid her blushes, as she nestled close to her little one, now smiling in her sleep.

The Impish Tale of

THE FAIRY PONIES

Y ou will not be surprised to learn that fairy ponies are very small. Even the largest ones are not much bigger than a mouse. They are, of course, the perfect size for fairies, but strangely enough, you never, ever see a fairy riding a pony.

Some professors, writing on this subject, claim the reason is that, as fairies have wings, they do not need to ride. Flying is quicker and more convenient, they say.

I can tell you now that professors, for all their learning and reading, know almost nothing about fairies. The fact that these little people do not ride fairy ponies has nothing to do with flying. It has everything to do with the ponies themselves.

You see, long ago, in the days when the first fairies flitted around the earth, it didn't occur to them to try to ride on the back of an animal. I mean, you don't see rabbits trying to hitch a ride on the backs of cows, do you? Some creatures carry their little ones, it is true, but that's different. Anyway, in those days, fairies flew and ponies trotted and that was the end of the matter.

But the first human beings were not able to fly. They soon got fed up with walking around on their own two feet. It took them ages to go anywhere, and it was annoying that other animals could run faster and sometimes seemed to be laughing at the slow and lumbering humans.

One fine day, it suddenly occurred to a young human that it might be easier to let a faster animal take the strain. Of course, that wasn't the end of the story. Several very surprised ponies and a lot of bruised bottoms later, the idea was still not very practical. Human beings, however, though slow, can be determined. In the end, they found out how to ride.

The fairies, who had watched all this with interest—and, it must be confessed, a great deal of laughter—became more thoughtful. If humans could do it, why shouldn't fairies? The little people looked at fairy ponies with new eyes.

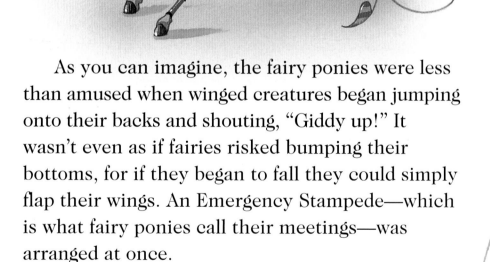

As you can imagine, the fairy ponies were less than amused when winged creatures began jumping onto their backs and shouting, "Giddy up!" It wasn't even as if fairies risked bumping their bottoms, for if they began to fall they could simply flap their wings. An Emergency Stampede—which is what fairy ponies call their meetings—was arranged at once.

"We can't have this!" neighed a famous fairy pony. "Where will it end? Before we know it, we'll be at the beck and call of those two-legged creatures all the time."

"You're right!" snuffled an elderly pony. "But what can we do to stop it? They have a huge advantage with their wings and their little fingers. They can land on your back and tangle their hands in your mane before you have a chance to spring and prance to get them off. We are simply no match for those cunning little creatures."

"I can't believe that," replied the first neigher, and his friends nodded their heads and whinnied in agreement. "We need to find their weak point, that's all."

"The only real weakness of fairies," said another pony thoughtfully, "is that they are very proud and hate to look ridiculous. But I don't see how that helps us. They are not like humans who fall to the ground with a bump all the time."

But that gave the wisest, oldest pony of all an idea. Before long, his friends were rolling on the ground and laughing.

After that, whenever a fairy jumped onto a pony's back, the clever creature didn't neigh or rear up or jump sideways. He or she simply started trotting backwards! The fairies hated it. They looked silly and they knew it. It wasn't long, much to the fairy ponies' relief, before they dropped the whole idea.

So now you know why fairies never ride. Don't try to tell those professors. They'll never believe it!

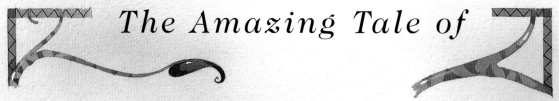

The Amazing Tale of
THE MUSICAL PONIES

Over the mountains and across the silvery sea is a land where flowers bloom and butterflies float on the scented air. There are feathery green trees, where beautiful birds settle by day and sleep by night. In sparkling streams, bright little fish flash and shine. Sunlit meadows stretch down to the deep blue sea. It is the loveliest place in the whole world. It is called Everlind.

And yet, although Everlind is the most peaceful and heavenly land you could imagine, you might not want to live there. You see, Everlind is silent. The birds do not sing. The wind does not sigh in the trees. The little streams do not chuckle and splash as they tumble over rocks. Even the sea is silent. It is very, very strange.

The tiny people who live in Everlind are perfectly happy. They are a little like elves, and even have pointy ears, but they are only for decoration. There is nothing to hear.

The Everlinders talk to each other with sign language. They have arguments and lullabies, poems and jokes, just as speaking people do. There is nothing they cannot tell each other. The Everlinders are happy in Everlind, which is just how it should be.

It was one day in late spring that everything changed in Everlind. To this day, no one knows why it happened.

A large family of tiny Everlinder people was having a picnic in a flowery meadow near a cool, deep lake. The children were playing in the grass while the grown-ups rested after lunch. Far away in the distance, a herd of the wild white ponies of Everlind were peacefully grazing. They drifted slowly nearer.

Several of the older Everlinders and a couple of the smallest had fallen asleep. The rest were playing games or chatting with their hands. In the middle of all this, in the silent sunshine, one of the white ponies drew near. He lifted up his head, opened his mouth, and sang.

Yes, he really sang. Music came out of his throat—and to our ears, it was a lovely sound, musical but deep, like the golden notes of a cello.

The confusion among the Everlinders was shocking to see. The sleepers woke up. The others stopped what they were doing and whirled around in astonishment. Then, with expressions of pain and disbelief, they clutched their ears and ran, as fast as they could, from the singing pony, gathering up their little ones but leaving all their belongings on the grass.

To the Everlinders, the noise was horrible. It seemed to travel right through their bodies, hurting them with its strangeness and power.

News of the terrible event spread quickly through Everlind. Meetings were held and votes were taken. A small party of Everlinders was chosen to go out and investigate what was happening. If only one pony was making the dreadful noise, perhaps something could be done.

The expedition was gone for two days. When it returned, its members were pale. Their hands trembled so much that they could hardly tell their friends what they had discovered.

At last the terrible truth became known. It was not only one pony that could sing. All the ponies were doing it. Sometimes, they sang together, and the sound, it seemed, was awful beyond description.

"What can we do?" asked the Everlinders.

"The world is going mad! We love our silent land. Now everything is changing."

They were terribly afraid. It was not only that strange, new sounds were invading their lives. Now, they no longer felt safe. If ponies could begin to sing, what else might happen? Would trees talk? Would butterflies chatter? Would houses laugh as they went by?

It was only a few weeks later that the second astonishing thing happened in Everlind. Visitors from another land arrived on the shore in boats. They were larger than the Everlinders but they seemed kind.

Although they, too, talked to each other with sounds, they soon began to learn to use signs to talk to the Everlinders. The tiny people, shocked by the musical ponies, were less surprised by the talking-out-loud people.

Pretty soon, the talking people became friends. The Everlinders showed them around the island—everywhere except the meadows where the singing ponies roamed.

"You won't want to go there," explained the tiny people. "It would hurt you to hear them."

But the visitors were curious. They asked to be taken to the meadows, and when their hosts refused, they set off by themselves.

The outsiders were enchanted. "These ponies are better than silver and gold!" they cried. "May we take some home with us? Their singing is glorious! They will be so admired."

"Take them all!" signed the Everlinders eagerly.

Silence returned to Everlind. The Everlinders were happy once more. And now you know why, although the singing ponies of Everlind are famous all over the world, the place that you will never ever find one is … Everlind.

The Moonstruck Tale of

THE PALACE PONIES

The King of Colomble was a proud man.
Everything in his palace had to be perfect.
Not surprisingly, it took him twenty years to find a
wife who came up to his high standards. She
turned out to be as vain and silly as her husband.

"My dear," she said at breakfast one morning,
"something must be done about the palace ponies."

"Really?" The King raised an inquiring
eyebrow. "But they are the finest that money can
buy. And their hoofs are polished daily."

"They are white," complained the Queen.
"A pretty shade of blue would be so much more
stylish. Surely you can arrange that, my dear?"

The King frowned. Blue ponies would certainly
look attractive. He promised to do what he could.

But the Royal Groom shook her head.

"It's impossible," she said. "The delicate skins
of these perfect ponies could never be dyed. And
there is no other way of making them blue."

When the King tried to argue, the Royal Groom
spoke even more firmly. "Blue dye would bring
them out in blisters and blotches," she said.
"Surely you don't want that!"

The King shuddered at the thought. Later that
day, he told the Queen what had happened. She
was not sympathetic.

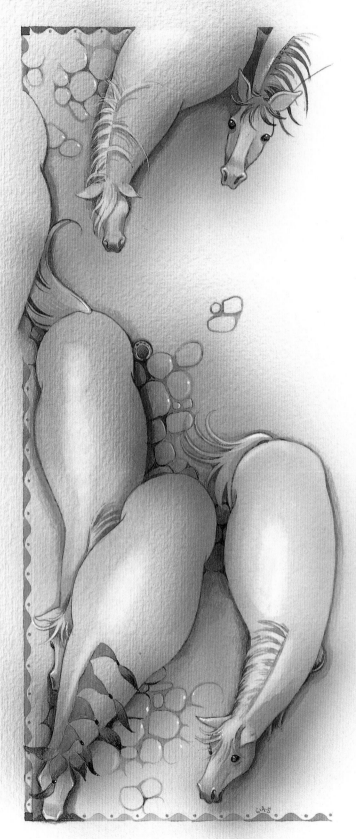

"Nonsense!" she cried. "I have the most sensitive skin in the world, and nothing has ever brought me out in blotches and blisters."

The King looked up in surprise, viewing his wife's golden ringlets with new eyes. "Do you mean…?" he began in horror.

"Certainly not!" cried the Queen, seeing that she had made a big mistake. "I will speak to the Royal Groom myself."

But that night, when she looked down from her bedroom window, the Queen had a most delightful surprise. Down in the palace courtyard, gleaming in the moonlight, were twelve ponies of the most perfect shade of pale blue. The Queen went to bed a happy woman.

The next morning, the Queen ordered her carriage. "And be sure it is pulled by the new, blue ponies," she said.

The Royal Groom came in person to speak to her mistress.

"Madam, there are no blue ponies in the stables," she said. "You are welcome to come and see for yourself."

Of course, the Queen protested. She insisted on searching every inch of the stables personally. Then she toured the extensive palace grounds. Not a single pale blue pony did she see.

The Queen had almost decided that her vision of blue ponies had been a dream when, that evening, she once more looked out of her window and saw the magical animals.

This time, the Queen wasted no time. She swept downstairs and into the courtyard, calling the Royal Groom from her bed above the stable as she went.

Out in the courtyard, the Queen beamed with satisfaction at the beautiful creatures stamping their hoofs in the moonlight.

"I suppose you will not tell me now that there are no blue ponies in the palace," she said triumphantly.

The Royal Groom opened her mouth to speak and closed it again. She knew that it was only the moonlight making the ponies appear blue, but she felt sure that the Queen would not want to be made to seem stupid—even if she was!

"You are right, Madam," she said at last. "I succeeded in finding a way of dyeing the ponies blue, but their skins are now so sensitive that they cannot go out in daylight. Only in the gentle moonlight are they safe from harm."

"I understand completely," said the Queen, reflecting that the time was fast approaching when she herself would look a great deal better by moonlight and candlelight than she would by the cruel light of day.

Ever since then, the most fashionable people in Colomble have slept by day and lived by night. Because they are also the silliest, vainest and most irritating people in Colomble, that suits the rest of the kingdom very well indeed. And the pale blue ponies of the palace keep the secret of their beauty to this day.

The Charming Tale of

THE PRETTIEST PONY

When Silver entered her new foal for the
Prettiest Pony Contest, she was sure that
little Blossom would win. None of the other pony-
mothers had such charming children.

But Silver was taking no chances. She sent a
special present of the best hay to one judge and
some particularly juicy carrots to the other.

"Bribing the judges is surely not allowed in the
rules," commented Major, her husband, over his
breakfast bran on the morning of the contest.

"Bribing?" cried Silver in injured tones. "Why, I've known old Racer and Fleet since I was a foal myself. I can give my old friends a small present if I want to, can't I?"

The proud mother spent hours combing her little daughter's mane and polishing her hoofs. She told the little one how to toss her head prettily and whinny in a ladylike manner when the judges came by.

At last, it was time for the contest. Blossom lined up with the other little ponies. The judges trotted solemnly to their places. But where were Racer and Fleet?

"I regret to announce," neighed the contest organizer, "that our esteemed judges are indisposed from over-indulgence in hay and carrots— let that be a lesson to you, little ones—and are unable to be with us this afternoon. Instead, Prancer and Posy have agreed to judge our contest.

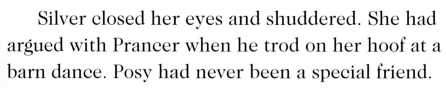

Silver closed her eyes and shuddered. She had argued with Prancer when he trod on her hoof at a barn dance. Posy had never been a special friend.

"We may as well go home," whispered Silver to her husband.

"Just wait and see," said Major.

You can imagine how delighted Silver was when her beloved daughter won first prize.

"But I don't understand it," she said to her husband as the family trotted home that evening. "I know that Prancer and Posy don't like me at all. Wait a minute, Major, did you have a word with them? Or perhaps send them a little something?"

Major stamped his hoof and laughed. "There's a much simpler explanation, my dear," he said.

"What? What?" cried Silver. "I must know!"

Major looked fondly at his little daughter. "It's quite plain for anyone to see," he said proudly. "Blossom really is the prettiest pony of all."

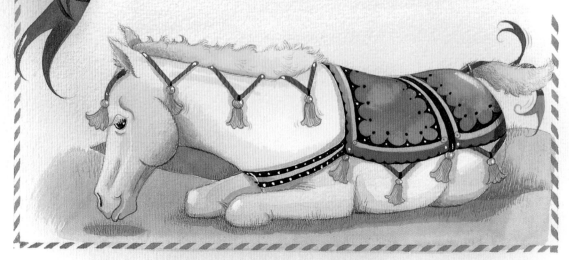